Collect all the PIPER REED books

(formerly *Piper Reed, the Great Gypsy*)

(formerly *Piper Reed Gets a Job*)

PIPER REED, RODEO STAR

(COMING SOON!)

KIMBERLY WILLIS HOLT

Piper Reed
CAMPFIRE
GIRL

Illustrated by

CHRISTINE DAVENIER

Christy Ottaviano Books

HENRY HOLT AND COMPANY

NEW YORK

Henry Holt and Company, LLC
Publishers since 1866
175 Fifth Avenue
New York, New York 10010
www.HenryHoltKids.com

Library of Congress Cataloging-in-Publication Data
Holt, Kimberly Willis.
Piper Reed , campfire girl / Kimberly Willis Holt ; illustrated by Christine Davenier.—1st ed.
        p.   cm.
"Christy Ottaviano Books"
Summary: Fifth-grader Piper and her sisters are thrilled about their first-ever
camping trip until they learn it will be at Halloween, but other Navy families join them,
including an annoying new member of the Gypsy Club.
ISBN 978-0-8050-9006-2
[1. Camping—Fiction. 2. Clubs—Fiction. 3. Halloween—Fiction.
4. Family life—Florida—Fiction. 5. United States. Navy—Fiction.
6. Pensacola (Fla.)—Fiction.] I. Davenier, Christine, ill. II. Title.
PZ7.H74023Pig 2010   [Fic]—dc22   2009050765

First Edition—2010
Printed in August 2010 in the United States of America by
R. R. Donnelley & Sons Company, Harrisonburg, Virginia

1   3   5   7   9   10   8   6   4   2

For the Retreat Girls—
Kathi Appelt, Rebecca Kai Dotlich,
Jeanette Ingold, and Lola Schaefer:
Love and Pie

—K. W. H.

PIPER REED

CAMPFIRE
GIRL

CONTENTS

1 ALL ABOUT STANLEY ~~~~~~~~~~~~ 1

2 THE NEW HAMPSHIRES ~~~~~~~~ 17

3 THE BIG SURPRISE ~~~~~~~~~~ 32

4 RENDEZVOUS IN YAZOO ~~~~~~~ 47

5 CAMP CHIC-A-DEE ~~~~~~~~~~~ 60

6   GONE FISHING 〜〜〜〜〜〜〜〜 76

7   PROJECT STANLEY 〜〜〜〜〜〜 91

8   NO EASY JOB 〜〜〜〜〜〜〜〜 101

9   CAMPSITE HALLOWEEN 〜〜〜〜 111

10   CALLING BRUNA 〜〜〜〜〜〜〜 133

11   HAPPY TRAILS 〜〜〜〜〜〜〜〜 141

1

~~~

ALL ABOUT STANLEY

Halloween was just two weeks away. Trick-or-treating and jack-o'-lanterns—that was all I could think about. But I still hadn't decided on my costume. I thought about dressing as a Blue Angel pilot for the U.S. Navy since that's what I planned to be when I grew up. But I didn't own a Blue Angel's uniform.

On the way to school, I asked, "Do you think the base is going to do anything special for Halloween?"

We lived at NAS Pensacola because our dad was a Navy chief.

"I'm going to be someone that I've never been before," my little sister, Sam, said.

"Who?"

"Princess Elizabeth."

"What's new about that?" I asked. "You're a princess every year." Sam would use any excuse to wear her crown.

Sam frowned. "I've never been Princess Elizabeth before."

"I thought she was Queen Elizabeth." I knew some things about the royal family.

"Queens have to be princesses first," said Sam.

"What are you going to be?" I asked Tori.

My big sister was sitting in the front seat with Mom. We had to drop her off at the middle school before Mom drove us to the elementary school where we went and where she worked as the art teacher.

Tori didn't answer me so I spoke louder. "Well, what are you going to be?"

She turned around and rolled her eyes. "Piper, Halloween is for little kids. I'm almost thirteen. I don't do dress up."

"You mean you have to stop having fun when you're a teenager?" I was sure glad I was in fifth

grade. That meant I still had a few good years left.

"I'll stay home and give out the candy," Tori said.

"Gosh," I said, "the trick-or-treaters won't stand a chance." My sister loved to eat. She'd probably empty the candy bowl before the first goblin rang our doorbell.

Tori glared at me. "Piper Reed, you're mean." Then her head snapped in Mom's direction. "Mom!"

Mom wasn't a morning person. She needed coffee. Lots of coffee. She probably didn't hear one word I said, but she went into her warning tone. "Girls, behave. It's too early for this."

Before the bell rang I met the other Gypsy Club members. We gathered in our usual spot near the front of the school sign. The twins, Michael and Nicole, were already there. But this time there was someone else standing in our circle—a boy with hair that stuck straight up like he forgot to comb it.

Hailey hopped off the bus and raced across the school yard. When she caught up with me, she asked, "Who's that boy?"

"I don't know, but he's in our meeting place."

"Hi, Piper." Nicole flashed her braces. She must have gone to the orthodontist because yesterday her rubber bands were fuchsia. Today she wore orange and black ones.

"Hi," I said, but I was staring at the new kid. He had the thickest glasses I'd ever seen on anyone.

"This is Stanley Hampshire," Michael said. "He just moved here." He punched Stanley's shoulder. He acted like Stanley was his new best friend.

"Oh," I said. "Hi, Stanley. I'm sorry, but this is a Gypsy Club meeting spot."

Hailey snapped, "Piper, you're mean!"

That was the second time I'd heard that today and the morning bell hadn't even rang yet. Hailey was right. I was being mean. My dad was a Navy chief. I knew what it was like being the new kid. I'd moved a zillion times.

"I . . . I was thinking," Michael stammered. "I was thinking Stanley could be in our Gypsy Club."

I gave Stanley a good look over. I'd only lived in Pensacola a year. That first day was hard until I started the Gypsy Club.

"He meets all the qualifications," Michael said. "His dad is in the Navy. He moves a lot, too. And he already knows the Gypsy Club creed."

"What?" I yelled.

Everyone stared at me.

"You taught him the Gypsy Club creed without asking permission of your fellow Gypsy Club members?"

Michael folded his arms across his chest. "I don't remember that being a rule."

"Well, some rules shouldn't have to be spoken."

"Am I supposed to read your mind?"

Stanley stared down at the ground. He was probably real smart and read a lot. Smart people had to wear glasses because they wore out their eyes from reading all those books. That meant my eyes had a lifetime guarantee.

Nicole spoke up. "I don't see anything wrong with Stanley being in the Gypsy Club. It's hard to be new and make friends."

Without saying a word, Stanley glanced around the playground. I guess he was the silent type. The smart, silent type, who had replaced me as Michael's best friend.

Everyone scowled at me. My face burned. I knew when I was outnumbered. Sometimes even a captain has to listen to her soldiers. I saluted him. "Welcome to the Gypsy Club, Stanley!"

All of a sudden, Stanley opened his mouth real wide and shouted, "Get off the bus!"

Then he started to talk very fast. "I mean thanks. You're really not going to regret this. I've never been a member of a club before, but I think I'll be good at it. I once was in the Boy Scouts of America. That's not really a club. The Boy Scouts of America is an organization, but, anyway, I was only a member for a short while. I never earned a badge though. I wanted to earn the knot-tying badge. I really wanted that one bad because my dad is a sailor. I mean, he's an officer, but he sails for a hobby. I go with him sometimes, but I'm not very good at it. Now my brother, Simon—"

The school bell rang. Kids raced by us and went inside the building. I usually dreaded that sound, but now I knew what it meant to be saved by the bell!

Nicole took off for her class while Hailey and

I followed the boys. I wasn't sure about this new kid, Stanley. He'd already weaseled his way into the Gypsy Club. Now he was going to be in my class, too. That added up to a lot of Stanley Hampshire. At least he lived in the officer housing instead of the enlisted housing. That way I wouldn't be bumping into him on my street.

As usual Ms. Gordon made a big to-do about Stanley being the new kid. She always made it sound like a new kid was a gift to our class.

"Students," she said, "may I present Stanley Hampshire. He moved here from Norfolk, Virginia. Stanley, would you like to tell us a little about yourself?"

Uh-oh. For a teacher, Ms. Gordon sure had a lot to learn.

Stanley stood like he was running for mayor of Pensacola, Florida. He pushed up his glasses.

He cleared his throat. "Well, my name is Stanley Hampshire, but you already know that. I was born in Germany, but I don't remember a thing about it because we moved by the time I was six months old, although my mom said I lived there long enough to develop a taste for Wiener schnitzel. But my dad says that's a fairy tale. Next we moved to Bremerton, Washington, and apparently we could see Mount Rainier from our backyard, but I don't remember that either because we moved before I was three. Then after that—"

Ms. Gordon said, "Okay, Stanley, thank you."

"But I didn't get to tell you about the other

places I lived or what my favorite color is or my favorite television show."

Ms. Gordon's right eyelid started twitching. "That's quite all right, Stanley. We need to start our day."

Stanley looked disappointed. "Well, all right, if you say so." He sat down.

Right off, I could see that I was going to have to make a new rule for the Gypsy Club—Gypsy Club members must not be blabbermouths.

At lunch, Michael, Hailey, Nicole, and I learned everything the rest of the class missed.

Stanley had also lived in Groton, Connecticut, and in Hawaii. His favorite color was blue, not the blue of the sky but the blue on his fourth-grade geography textbook. He had two brothers and, according to Stanley, his oldest brother was the smartest human being in the world. "Simon will probably be president of the United States someday."

Stanley told us his favorite song was "Yankee Doodle." How could my favorite song be the same as his?

"'Yankee Doodle' makes me want to spin," said Stanley.

Hailey was about to take a bite when he said that. She put her sandwich down and asked, "Why?"

Stanley shrugged. "Beats me. I guess the rhythm makes me want to spin."

"'Yankee Doodle' makes me want to march," said Nicole.

"That's because 'Yankee Doodle' is a marching song," I said.

"If you say so," said Stanley. He chomped on his carrot and swallowed quickly. I knew what was coming next. More about Stanley Hampshire.

Right after lunch, Ms. Mitchell came into our classroom. I glanced at the clock. It was one thirty. I had already been to her room. She must miss me. Every morning I go to Ms. Mitchell's room. While the other kids have to read together in our classroom, I get to read alone with Ms. Mitchell. That's because I have dyslexia.

I love Ms. Mitchell's room. It has an orange beanbag chair I sit in while I read. And she stashes stickers in her drawer—zillions of stickers. She lets me pick out a sticker for my notebook every time I read good . . . I mean, read well. That means I get a sticker every day because I've improved a lot since I started working with her last year. I grabbed my notebook and went to meet her at the front of the class.

"Hi, Piper," Ms. Mitchell said, smiling.

"Sit down, Piper," Ms. Gordon said.

"But I need to go to Ms. Mitchell's class," I told Ms. Gordon.

"Piper, I'm afraid it's not your turn," Ms. Mitchell said.

"But—"

Ms. Gordon's eye twitched. "Piper, please return to your seat." Then she said, "Stanley Hampshire, please come here and meet Ms. Mitchell."

Stanley stood and we passed each other on my return to my seat.

Ms. Gordon said, "Stanley Hampshire, this is your reading teacher, Ms. Mitchell."

Then Ms. Mitchell—my Ms. Mitchell— held out her hand. "Stanley, I can't wait to get to know you."

Uh-oh.

"Well," Stanley started, "I was born in Germany, which I don't remember a thing about because we moved when I was six months—"

"That's enough, Stanley," Ms. Gordon said. "You'll have plenty of time this year to tell Ms.

Mitchell about yourself. For now it's time to read."

"But—"

"Go along now." Even from where I sat, I could see both of Ms. Gordon's eyes twitch.

2

THE NEW HAMPSHIRES

After school, Sam and I waited for Mom at the van. We always waited until the buses left and Mom was finished in her room. One by one, the yellow buses pulled away from the curb and left the parking lot. The roar of engines faded away, and the school grounds became as quiet as a church on Monday.

A few minutes later what looked like a box with legs moved toward us. It was Mom. I ran up to help her.

"Thanks, Piper," Mom said as I grabbed hold of one side of the box.

I peeked inside. Dried flower petals, seeds,

and plastic cups—stuff we'd used for our spring art projects.

"I need to make room in my cabinets for this year's projects," Mom said.

We put the box in the back of the van and headed to Tori's middle school.

On the way, Mom asked Sam, "What did you do today?"

"We read a book about falling leaves and talked about patterns, but we didn't talk about Halloween."

"You can talk about it now," Mom said. "How was your day, Piper?"

"Okay, I guess." Then I added, "We have a new boy."

"What's his name?" Mom asked.

"Stanley."

"Tell me about him." Mom liked to know about the new students before she met them in art class. She said she wanted to make them feel as special as she hoped teachers made us feel every time we moved to a new school.

"Oh, nothing interesting."

"Just remember," Mom said. "You know what it's like to be new."

"I let him be in the Gypsy Club."

"That's the Gypsy spirit!" Mom said. "I'm proud of you."

At least someone thought I'd done the right thing. Making Stanley a Gypsy Club member was probably the biggest mistake of my life. But I'd have to live with it.

Sam perked up. "We have a new boy, too. I almost forgot."

"What's his name?" Mom asked.

"Kirby. Kirby Hampshire."

"Hampshire?" I asked. "His last name is Hampshire?" Then I remembered Stanley said he had two brothers. And how could I forget Simon, the perfect older brother?

"Yes," Sam said. "Like *New* Hampshire. Only it's Kirby Hampshire."

"Well, I hope he talks less than his brother Stanley."

"He doesn't talk at all. Unless the teacher talks to him, then his face turns red."

"Lucky you," I muttered. Figures. I had to get the Hampshire kid who couldn't shut up.

At the middle school, Tori floated into the car with a silly grin. That could mean one of two things. Either she got a poem published in the school paper or she had a new crush.

"Hi, Tori," Mom said. "Anything special happen today?"

"Nothing much." She stared out the window. "Well, we did get a new student."

"Oh," Mom said. "Seems this is the day for new students."

"What's his name?" I asked. "Simon Hampshire?"

Tori turned around, her eyes popping wide. "How did you know that?"

"I'll bet he has two brothers—Kirby and Stanley." Seems Hampshires were taking over Pensacola, Florida.

"I have no idea," Tori said smugly. "I just know Simon is the smartest guy I've ever met. He's in all of my honors classes."

Tori never missed a chance to remind me that she was a brain. Actually my sister was smart. She read books all the time, but she hadn't worn out her eyes yet. I guess Tori pretty much shot down my theory that everyone who was smart wore glasses.

Tori said, "Simon was the student body president at his last school in Norfolk, and he's already joined three clubs at our school. This is his first day. There's no telling what he'll accomplish by the end of the week. He's even joined the Poetry Club."

"Hmm," I said. "Aren't *you* a member of the Poetry Club?"

Tori ignored me.

"He loves Ted Kooser's poems."

"Ted who?" I asked.

Tori snapped her tongue against the roof of her mouth. "Good grief, he won a Pulitzer and was the Poet Laureate of the United States."

"Of course, how could I forget that," I said under my breath.

"What is a poet laureate?" Sam asked.

Tori's voice softened. She usually reserved her mean voice for lucky me. "It's an honor given to a gifted poet."

"Oh," Sam said. "Sort of like someone who wins the spelling bee?"

Sam was a spelling bee prodigy and she never let us forget it.

We reached the base and the gate guard signaled us through. I turned and saluted him as we rode by.

When we got out of the car, our three-year-old neighbor, Brady, waved from his front yard. "Hi, Piper!"

"Hi, Brady."

"Hi, Sam!"

"Hi, Brady."

Tori stood with her books in her hands, waiting. Finally she said, "Hi, Brady."

Brady walked all the way over to the edge of our yards where his mom, Yolanda, told him he must not step over without her permission.

"Hey, Sam, guess what I'm going to be for twick-or-tweat?"

Tori shook her head and walked toward the house. "I swear that kid doesn't like me. What have I ever done to him?"

Brady might be only three, but he knows a grump when he sees one.

"Twee guesses, Sam!" Brady said.

"A ghost?" Sam asked.

"Nope."

"A vampire?" I asked.

Brady giggled. "No, silly. One more guess."

"How about the president of the United States of America?" Sam asked.

Brady raised his chin and stared straight at Sam. "A pwince."

"A prince?" Sam shrieked. She acted like he'd yanked the crown right off her head.

"Yep." Brady nodded "A pwince."

"Oh." Sam seemed lost for words. Then she told him, "It's really hard to be a member of the royal family. There's a lot of responsibilities."

"Like what?" I asked.

Sam frowned at me. "You have no idea."

"Sam, we're talking about Halloween," I said.

"It's not like he wants to take over a country."

Brady stepped over the imaginary line. Then, as if he remembered, he jumped back. "Hey, Sam?"

"What?" she asked.

"Can I be *your* pwince?"

Sam put her finger to her chin. "I'll have to think about it."

"Just tell him *yes*," I said. "Yes, he can be your prince."

"I told him I'd think about it, didn't I?" Sam marched into the house.

I started to follow her, then I turned and told Brady, "You're going to make a great prince."

Inside the house, Sam picked up the container of fish flakes. She stood on her tiptoes as she sprinkled flakes into her goldfish Peaches the Second's bowl.

I couldn't believe how snotty she was about Brady wanting to be her prince for Halloween.

Sam put the container down with a thump. "I'm thinking about it."

Bruna came over and stared up at me with a look that told me she wanted to go outside.

I grabbed her leash and took her for a walk.

We left our street and headed for the base park. Two weeks until Halloween and I still hadn't figured out my costume. All I knew was that I wanted to be something different. Something no one would think of in a million years. Whenever I thought really hard about something, I entered a dreamlike world. Mom did that, too. Once she forgot and left the car running in the garage for two hours. Chief said we were lucky the house didn't blow up.

What could I be for Halloween? A witch? Nah, too ordinary. A Blue Angel pilot? I'd need a real uniform. I kept thinking of the possibilities.

And that's how it happened.

That's how I walked smack into Stanley Hampshire like he was nothing but air. He fell flat on his back.

I looked down. "Stanley?"

He looked up. "That sure is a cute dog you have. I always wanted a dog, but my dad says I can't have one because I'd forget to feed it, but I'm certain I wouldn't. Although I did forget to eat breakfast once. But I was starving by the time lunch came around and I've never forgotten to eat a—"

"Stanley, why don't you shut up—I mean *get* up?" I held out my hand to him.

Bruna licked his knobby knees. "Stanley, I have to get home. My mom doesn't know where I am." That wasn't a lie. I'd forgotten to tell her. I dashed away, but Stanley hollered, "Hey, when's the next Gypsy Club meeting?"

I could have pretended not to have heard. Instead I hollered, "Saturday at my house."

"What's your address?" he asked.

And then I told him. Great! Now Stanley Hampshire knew where I lived.

3

THE BIG SURPRISE

Mom was on a health-food kick. That night she fixed tofu stir-fry. Last week we had steamed fish and vegetables and eggplant lasagna with fake cheese.

It was my turn to set the table. While I tried to remember which side of the plate to place the napkins, I heard Mom on the phone with Chief. Before she hung up, she said, "That's a wonderful idea, Karl. The girls will love it."

What were we going to love? A trip to

Disney? Paris? Maybe we were going to get a house with four bedrooms. Then I wouldn't have to share a room with Sam anymore. Or maybe we were going to a haunted house for Halloween. Before or after trick-or-treating, of course.

After Chief came home, we sat for dinner. I could hardly eat because I was so excited. I looked down at my plate and stirred the slices of rubbery tofu into the cabbage, celery, and bean sprouts.

Finally Chief said, "Girls—"

I dropped my chopsticks. "He's got something exciting to tell us," I blurted.

Chief glanced toward Mom, "Did you already tell them, Edie?"

"No," she said, looking confused.

"We're going camping," he announced.

"Uncle Leo is letting us borrow his Airstream," Mom added.

"Get off the bus!" I hollered. I stared down at my plate. "I'm so excited, I can't eat another bite."

Mom's left eyebrow shot up.

"But it's delicious," I quickly added.

Tori wrinkled her nose. "Camping? Do you mean, like, in the great outdoors?"

"Is there any other kind of camping?" I asked. Tori's idea for camping was sitting by the pool with a bag of chocolate-dipped Oreos.

"I can't wait!" Sam said. "I've never been camping before."

"You can't wear your crown," I told her. Sam used to wear her crown everywhere until she got teased at school when we moved to Pensacola.

Sam lowered her eyebrows, frowning. "I wouldn't wear my crown camping."

I'd never camped either. Sleeping on Grandma and Grandpa Reed's screened porch was the closest I'd been to camping. I didn't know I wanted to go so badly until Chief mentioned it.

"When are we going?" I asked him.

"In two weeks. Y'all have a three-day break. It will be perfect. There's a park a few hours away in Alabama. Hopefully it will be a little cooler by then."

Two weeks from now? Why did that sound familiar?

Sam's eyes grew wide. "But two weeks from now is Halloween."

Bingo!

Tears welled up in Sam's eyes. "We can't miss Halloween."

"Girls," Chief said, "there will be other Halloweens. This is

a chance to go fishing and sit around a campfire. Breathe some fresh air."

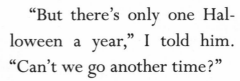

"But there's only one Halloween a year," I told him. "Can't we go another time?"

Tori sighed.

Chief's shoulders lowered and he sighed. He reminded me of a balloon losing air. "Girls, if I'd known you'd feel this way I wouldn't have gone through so much trouble. Now it's too late to back out."

"Why is it too late?" I asked.

"I've already paid a deposit on the campsite. Plus I've arranged to meet your uncle halfway for the trailer."

"But we can't miss trick-or-treating," Sam said. "We'll miss the candy."

"We'll buy some candy and take it camping," Mom said.

"It's not the same," I told her. "Plus, we'd have to hide it from Tori."

Tori narrowed her eyes at me, and Mom started to speak, but I beat her to it. "Sorry."

Mom put down her fork and leaned over her plate. "There are going to be other kids there."

"Who?" Tori asked.

"Nicole and Michael's family, and Isabel and Abe."

"Is Brady getting to stay and go trick-or-treating?" Sam asked.

"Brady is going camping," Mom said. "Isabel and Abe wouldn't leave him behind."

Sam sighed. "Brady will cry. He was going to be my prince."

I looked at her.

Sam glared back. "I said I would think about it."

"Great," Tori said. "A bunch of little kids and no one for me."

"I'd let you invite a friend, Tori," Mom said, "but we'll barely have enough room as it is. Uncle Leo's Airstream sleeps four comfortably. And there's five of us."

"How about Bruna?" I asked.

"Well," Chief said, "we thought about boarding her at the kennel. That way we wouldn't have to worry about her."

"I'll watch her," I said. I didn't want Bruna to go to the kennel.

"I'll help," Tori said. "Since I can't take any friends."

"Do you girls know what a responsibility that will be?" Chief asked. "There's a leash policy so you can't let her roam loose."

"No problem," I said. I glanced at Tori.

"We'll take shifts," Tori said.

Chief nodded. "Okay. If you're both fine with that, I'll make a schedule list."

"How about Peaches the Second?" Sam asked.

"Peaches will be fine," said Mom. "She's a goldfish. We'll feed her a little extra before we leave."

Sam folded her arms across her chest. "That's not fair. Bruna can go camping, but not Peaches the Second. Just because she's a fish?"

Mom sighed and gazed at Chief across the table. "Who would have thought camping would be so complicated?" Then she turned her focus to Sam. "How about if I ask Mr. Sanchez at the pet store? He probably wouldn't mind one more fish."

Sam nodded. "Okay, if I have to go camping and miss trick-or-treating."

I should've been excited, but I wasn't. Even

though part of the Gypsy Club would be there, I didn't want to miss trick-or-treating. And besides, the way Tori talked, I had only a few Halloweens left. The Gypsy Club had a new mission for the next meeting. We had to figure out a way to change our parents' mind about ruining Halloween.

Saturday, Stanley showed up two hours early for the Gypsy Club meeting. Mom and Chief liked to sleep late on Saturdays, so Mom wasn't so happy when Stanley rang the doorbell at eight o'clock in the morning.

The doorbell woke me, too. I slipped on my robe and walked into the living room. Leaning against the doorway, Mom listened to Stanley tell his story. "And then we moved to Norfolk, Virginia, where I learned to ride a bike and . . ."

When Mom noticed me, she muffled a yawn and motioned me over. "Piper, Stanley is here for the meeting."

"Stanley," I said, "it doesn't start until ten o'clock."

"Simon says it's better to be early than late."

I was really beginning to dislike this Simon and I hadn't even met him.

Mom rubbed her eyes. "Stanley, why don't you wait in the living room while Piper changes her clothes. Have you eaten breakfast?"

"I had a Pop-Tart, but I could always eat."

"Why don't you stay? Piper's dad makes the best pancakes."

"Well, if you insist . . ."

Great! I was stuck with Stanley for two whole hours before the rest of the club arrived. At breakfast I listened to his life story again as he repeated the saga for my family. Tori kept

her nose stuck in a poetry book the entire time that he talked. But Sam was fascinated.

"Did you ever live in England?" she wanted to know.

"No, but I've been to the Heathrow Airport," Stanley told her. Then he told her how he'd eaten sushi there, the kind that floated on little boats around the sushi bar.

Sam blinked. "Did you see any of the royal family at the airport?"

"No," Stanley said.

"Oh," Sam sounded disappointed. "Are you going trick-or-treating?"

Then Stanley said the worst thing he could have said. "Michael asked me to go on a camping trip."

Finally 10:00 arrived. We met in the new club tent in our backyard. We recited the Gypsy Club creed.

We are the Gypsies of land and sea.
We move from port to port.
We make friends everywhere we go.
And everywhere we go, we let people know
That we're the Gypsies of land and sea.

"Everyone in favor of starting the meeting?" I asked.

"Aye!"

"Any nays?"

Silence.

Then Stanley spoke. "I just wanted to say I'm very honored to be a part of the Gypsy Club. I prom—"

"Stanley," I said, "I'm sorry to cut you off, but we have to start our meeting now."

He looked down at the grass and pushed at his glasses.

"We're glad to have you, Stanley," I said. "Now about this camping trip. All in favor of trying to convince our parents that another weekend would be better?" I said, "Aye!"

Hailey said, "Aye!"

Nicole said, "Aye!"

Michael said, "Aye!"

Stanley didn't say anything.

I couldn't believe what was happening. I slowly asked, "Any nays?"

Stanley pointed his arm toward the ceiling. "Nay."

"What?" we all asked.

"I want to go camping. I've only been once. With the Boy Scouts. And I wasn't very good at it then. I wanted to earn that campfire badge, but I didn't."

"Stanley," I told him, "we don't earn badges in the Gypsy Club."

"Maybe you should," he said. "We could have special shirts and as we earn badges we could have them sewn on the collars. Then when people asked about them we could tell them how we earned them. We could make it challenging to earn them, but not too hard. We could . . ."

I stared out the window as he went on and on. My head pounded. My stomach felt queasy. Stanley Hampshire was ruining my life.

4

RENDEZVOUS IN YAZOO

We were going camping. Halloween wouldn't happen this year. Sam pouted, but it didn't change Chief's mind. Yolanda told Mom that Brady cried when he found out he would miss out on his very first trick-or-treating.

A few nights after Chief's announcement, Sam and I lay in our beds, wide awake. Sam said, "I wonder what will happen when kids come to our door and no one answers."

That wasn't hard to figure out. I told her,

"They'll turn around, leave, and go to the next house."

"But Brady's family isn't going to be home either."

I sighed. "Then they'll turn around, leave, and go to the next house."

"But—"

"Sam, I'm trying to sleep."

But I couldn't sleep. My mind was on Halloween, too. One of my friends in San Diego said they'd moved during Halloween. Since

they were staying at a hotel, their mom let them dress up in their costumes and go to the mall. The awesome surprise was that all the stores gave out candy. So they trick-or-treated store-to-store. Turned out, Halloween happened after all. That's when it came to me—my big idea.

The next day I called for an emergency Gypsy Club meeting at recess. After we gathered, Stanley opened his mouth as if a ton of words were going to tumble out. I held up my hand to stop his words.

Stanley shut his mouth.

I felt like Superman stopping bullets.

"I have an idea," I told them. "If we can't stay home and trick-or-treat, who says that we can't celebrate Halloween while we camp?"

Silence.

The entire Gypsy Club stared at me as if I'd

said something stupid. Then all together they yelled, "Get off the bus!"

At home, everyone made lists. Well, everyone but Mom. She hated lists, especially since Chief tried to make lists for her.

<u>Chief's List</u>
1. Lanterns
2. Bug repellent
3. Tackle box
4. Rods and reels
5. Bait
6. Pop-up chairs
7. Charcoal
8. Lighter fluid and matches

<u>Tori's List</u>
1. Journal
2. Notebooks
3. Book of poems by Ted Kooser
4. Sunglasses

<u>Sam's List</u>

1. Crown
2. Costume
3. Magic wand

<u>My List</u>

1. Candy
2. Sheets for ghosts
3. Pumpkins
4. Apples
5. Masks

I still wasn't sure what I was going to be for Halloween, but I decided I'd make it when I got to the campgrounds. So I added to my list:

6. Scissors
7. Paints
8. Muslin
9. Needle
10. Thread

Then I thought about Bruna. She needed

treats. Not just any treats—her favorite treats.

11. Liver Lumps

The plan was to drive in our van and meet Uncle Leo at the halfway point in Yazoo, Alabama, while everyone else headed to the campgrounds. Uncle Leo would meet us with the trailer at 0900 hours in the post office parking lot. After we hitched the trailer to our van, we'd take off and meet up with everyone else at the campgrounds in time for lunch.

All the families met at dawn at the base entrance so that we could caravan to Yazoo.

Hailey and Stanley were with Michael and Nicole because they had a huge camping trailer that slept six. Brady's family took a pop-up tent that they'd rented for the weekend.

Tori and Sam dozed, but I was wide awake. I sat in the back seat by myself. Michael's family's RV was behind us, and since Michael was sitting in the front seat with his dad, I turned around and stuck out my tongue.

Then Michael crossed his eyes and touched his nose with his tongue. I still hadn't learned to do that. Michael was the Freaky Face Champion.

The first hour on the road flew by, but even making freaky faces gets boring. Not to mention my tongue became sore.

When we arrived at Yazoo, we waved good-bye to everyone else. Then we pulled into the post office parking lot. No Uncle Leo.

"Oh, dear," Mom said. "I was afraid of this."

"There are five minutes until 0900, Edie," Chief said. "Give him a chance."

Mom sighed. "We're talking about Leo. Remember, he has a terrible sense of direction."

"Why doesn't he use a GPS?" I asked.

Mom shook her head. "Piper, Uncle Leo wouldn't know how to program a GPS."

"What do you expect?" Tori said. "He's the absent-minded professor."

"I've never been absent," Sam said.

"Yes, you have," I told her. "Remember when we moved from San Diego last year? You missed a week of school."

"Well, I haven't been absent this year."

"It's only October. You might get some terrible disease like the creepy crawly disease."

"What's the creepy crawly disease?" she asked.

"You can only catch it around Halloween time," I told her.

To my surprise, Tori joined in. "Yes, that's right. You break out in pink spots all over your body."

"Well, I don't plan to get it," Sam said. "I'm going to be very careful and wash my hands a hundred times a day with soap."

"Good luck!" I told her.

Tori winked at me. "Yep. Good luck."

While we waited, I counted all the blue cars passing by.

"What time is it?" I asked.

"Ten o'clock," Mom said through gritted teeth. "He's lost. I just know it."

"Can't we call him?" I asked.

"Uncle Leo doesn't have a cell phone," Mom said. "He owned one once, but lost it. He said he never used it anyway."

When 11:00 arrived, I was thinking about hollering "Uncle Leo!" at the top of my lungs. It couldn't hurt. I was missing out on the fun. The other Gypsy Club members would be there by now and they'd be able to start putting our plan into action.

Thirty minutes later, I spotted an old beat-up truck with a silver trailer coming down the road. "There he is!" I hollered. "There's Uncle Leo!"

Then he drove right past the post office without even stopping.

"Was that him?" Sam asked.

"Yes." Mom and Chief groaned at the same time.

"Should we catch him?" I asked.

"Yazoo isn't that big. He'll turn around and figure it out," said Chief.

Mom frowned at Chief. "Don't bet on it."

Then I said, "Remember when Uncle Leo forgot how to get to Grandma's home?"

"And he grew up in that house," Tori said.

"Let's get out of the car, girls, so that he'll see us when he turns around."

We climbed out of the van and waited. Sure enough, ten minutes later Uncle Leo came back our way. We waved our arms high above our heads. We looked like we were signaling airplanes.

"Uncle Leo!" We yelled.

But Uncle Leo drove right on by.

Mom shook her head. "How could he miss us?"

Finally Chief said, "Let's catch him."

We climbed back into the van and Chief pressed the accelerator. Our van turned into a

NASCAR racecar. The wind blew through the open windows. Our hair and Bruna's ears flew like kite tails.

"Watch out, Karl," Mom said. "I wonder what the speed limit is in this little town?"

That's when our family met the sheriff of Yazoo, Alabama.

5

CAMP CHic-a-DEE

Chief pulled over to the side of the road.

"Are we going to jail?" asked Sam.

"Behave yourselves, girls," Chief said as the sheriff approached our van.

Chief pulled out his wallet and gave the sheriff his driver's license.

"Mr. Reed," the sheriff said, "we may be a small town, but we have laws."

"Yes, sir," Chief said. "I'm sorry. I was trying to catch up with——"

The sheriff held up his palm.

Chief stopped explaining. That hand trick must work on everyone.

Just as the sheriff handed a ticket to Chief, Uncle Leo drove up.

"Finally," I said.

Uncle Leo rolled down his window. "Excuse

me, sir. Could you tell me where I could find the Yazoo branch of the United States Post Office?"

Mom leaned over Chief and waved her hand out the window. "Leo! We're right here."

Uncle Leo squinted in our direction. "Oh, hi, Edie."

"Hi." Mom sounded mad.

"Hi, Karl."

"Hi, Leo."

"Hi, girls."

"Hi, Uncle Leo."

After the sheriff drove away, we headed to the post office. Uncle Leo helped Chief attach the Airstream to our van. Then we stopped at a diner for a soft drink before heading to the camp. My stomach growled as I watched the waitress serve hamburgers to another group. But Mom wouldn't let us order anything, except a drink, because she had told Yolanda we'd be there by lunchtime. I gulped down my cola while Mom and Chief asked Uncle Leo about Grandma and Grandpa Morris. But Uncle Leo always seemed to answer by telling them something else about hummingbirds. Most people are interested in all kinds of things. Not Uncle Leo. He's interested in only one thing—hummingbirds. Uncle Leo is a hummingbird expert. He's even traveled around the world studying different species, like the Stripe-tailed Hummingbird. Finally we took off for the campgrounds.

A couple of miles out of town, Chief glanced in the rearview mirror. Then he quickly looked again. "I hate to tell you this, Edie, but Leo is following us."

Chief pulled over on the shoulder of the road. Uncle Leo just waved and kept driving in the wrong direction.

"Maybe he wants to take the scenic route," I said.

Mom sighed. I thought it was bad having sisters like Tori and Sam. I guess even really smart people are dumb about some things. Uncle Leo knew everything about humming-birds, but he couldn't read a map or find his way back home.

At two o'clock we pulled into the camp-grounds.

"Where were you?" Hailey asked.

"We were worried," Nicole said.

"Did you stop at McDonald's?" Michael asked. "We had to eat turkey sandwiches. There's only one time a year that I want to eat turkey— Thanksgiving. And I don't even want it then."

"We didn't stop anywhere to eat," I said. "I'm starved." Even a turkey sandwich sounded delicious.

Mom shook her head and said, "Leo."

Chief explained what happened. Everyone laughed.

"I hope Uncle Leo finds his way home," I said.

"We tried waiting to eat as long as we could," Yolanda said, "but we got hungry. I don't know why we forgot to get each other's cell phone numbers."

While I ate my turkey sandwich, the other Gypsy Club members walked to the dock. I hurried and finished. Then I started to take off to join them at the lake.

"Piper, don't forget Bruna," Mom said.

I turned around and walked back.

Mom held out the leash. Bruna was at her feet, wagging her tail.

"You have the first shift," said Mom. "We didn't bring her so that she would be tied to a tree all day."

Bruna stretched up, resting her paws against my legs.

"Sit," I said.

Bruna sat.

Then I snapped the leash onto her collar. We ran toward the dock. The lake was sparkly with a few rowboats filled with people fishing. The trees were tall and thick around us. Before we got to the campgrounds, I could think only about Halloween. Now it was hard to think of anything but camping. I couldn't wait to go fishing and roast marshmallows.

Tori wandered up, holding her notebook. She was probably going to write some boring poems about water.

"Do you think we'll go fishing today?" Hailey asked.

"I don't know," I said. "It's kind of late. When Chief goes fishing he usually leaves early in the morning."

"My dad doesn't like to fish," Stanley said, "but he likes to sail."

"Does your brother like to sail?" Tori asked. Her voice sounded sweet and gooey. I almost didn't recognize it.

"Kirby doesn't like the water," said Stanley.

Tori shook her head. Her face turned red. "Not Kirby. S-Simon."

Stanley looked down at the water, fiddling with his glasses. "Oh, Simon is a good sailor. Simon is good at everything."

"Really?" Tori asked as if she hadn't gone

on and on about him all week. *Simon this.*
Simon that. I'd had about enough of Simon
Hampshire. Before long, he'd probably be the
youngest inventor of a new candy bar.

Stanley got real quiet and stared at the clouds.
I thought it was hard having two sisters who did
great in school, but I knew I could do a lot of
things they couldn't. I could draw better. I could
teach Bruna tricks. I could run and swim faster
than both of them together. But poor Stanley
didn't seem to be good at anything.

Stanley looked at Bruna. "Does your dog
bite?"

"Nope," I told him. "Want to make friends
with her?"

Stanley nodded.

"Let her sniff you first," I said.

"Huh?"

"Like this, Stanley." Michael put his hand
under Bruna's nose and Bruna smelled it.

Stanley slowly put his hand under Bruna's nose.

Bruna sniffed and sniffed at his fingers. Then she licked them.

Stanley laughed. "Hey, that tickles."

Nicole started to sneeze. "I'm allergic to dogs."

Michael sighed. "Yep, she's allergic to the whole world."

Nicole sneezed again. And again. She always

triple sneezed. Nicole was a champion sneezer.

Hailey tugged at Nicole's T-shirt. "Come on, Nicole. We'd better get you away from Bruna."

Nicole followed Hailey off the dock and toward the campgrounds. Someone had made a fire.

Keeping the entire Gypsy Club together and taking care of Bruna was going to be harder than I'd realized. Especially when one of the Gypsy Club members was allergic to dogs. I couldn't wait until it was Tori's turn.

I played with Bruna for a while, running back and forth along the lake. When she started panting and slowing down, I walked over to the campsite. I tied her leash to the leg of one of the picnic tables and joined my friends.

Tori stood smack in the middle of them. Tori, who thought she was too old for my friends. Tori, who thought the Gypsy Club was silly. Tori, who had no business sitting where I should have been sitting, announced, "We should write haikus."

"Hi who?" Stanley asked.

I knew what a haiku was because I had Tori Reed for a sister. I guess all her poetry talk dripped on me or something. "Haiku is a type of Japanese poem," I told him.

"It's usually about nature," Tori said, sounding just like the know-it-all she thinks she is.

"Doesn't each line have a certain number of syllables?" Hailey asked.

"Well," Tori said, "real haiku poets don't use this form, but to make it simple we could go with 5-7-5."

"Huh?" Stanley scratched his head.

"Five syllables for the first line," Hailey explained. "Then seven for the second, and five for the third."

"Oh, okay," Stanley said. "I think I remember Simon talking about haikus."

"Really?" The mere mention of Simon's name caused Tori's eyelashes to flutter. "What did Simon say about haikus?"

There was that name again. *Simon.*

Stanley shrugged. "Aw, I don't remember. But Simon won a poetry contest when we lived in Norfolk. They printed his poem in the newspaper and everything."

Sam rose on her tiptoes, trying to meet Stanley's eyes. "My picture has been in the newspaper."

"Well," Stanley said, "Simon's picture has been in the paper a lot for poetry and track and sailing and for earning the most Boy Scout badges and—"

"Okay, Stanley, we get the idea," I said. "Simon can do anything."

"Yeah," Stanley said, "he can. He'll probably be a famous author one day."

"No doubt," said Tori.

"I'm already an author," Sam said.

"You are?" Stanley asked, truly impressed. "What's your book? Maybe I've read it."

"*Princess Samantha, Ruler of the Fair Land of NAS Pensacola*."

"Oh," Stanley said. "I haven't read that."

"Most people haven't," I told him.

"Well, how about it?" Tori asked. "We don't have to work hard at it. We'll just let the haikus come to us like all good poetry. Pretty soon you'll find haikus everywhere."

We just stared at her.

Tori sighed and walked away.

That night we all sat around the campfire and roasted hot dogs on stakes that Chief and Michael's dad made from wire clothes hangers.

"Enjoy these hot dogs, folks," Chief said. "Tomorrow we're having fish."

"Are we going to get to catch them?" I asked.

"You bet," Chief said.

Sam wiggled. "I don't think I should fish. Peaches the Second wouldn't like it if I caught one of her relatives."

"Sam," I said, "there are no goldfish in that lake."

Sam folded her arms in front of her chest. "They could be distant relatives."

After dinner we slid marshmallows on the wire stakes and roasted them over the fire.

"Piper," Chief said, "be careful. I think your marshmallow is about to catch fire."

I took it out of the flames. It was burnt black to the crisp. "Ah, just like I like them. Crispy on the outside. Gooey on the inside."

Tori laughed. "Let's write a haiku about that. It could start: Gooey marshmallows."

Everyone was quiet for a moment. Then Nicole said, "Burnt black in the campfire flames."

"The way Piper likes," Stanley said.

Everyone clapped. Except me.

"That's great, Stanley," Tori said. "See? Writing haikus is exciting."

I should have known Tori would ruin this camping trip. She was going to squeeze out every bit of fun and use my friends to do it.

6

~~~~~

GONE FISHING

The next morning, it was still dark outside when Mom said, "Rise and shine, Gypsy girls."

I popped up. Even inside the trailer, I could smell last night's campfire. I slipped into my jeans and long-sleeved T-shirt.

Chief had to order Tori and Sam to get up. "Come on, team. The early bird catches the worm!"

Tori groaned. "Remind me, again, why I'm doing this."

Sam kept her eyes squeezed tight. "I don't want to catch a goldfish."

"No problem there," I told her. "If you find a goldfish in that lake, we've got another problem."

"Tori and Sam," Mom said, "fishing is fun. My fondest memories are fishing with my dad on Blue Lake. Leo never wanted to go, though. Maybe you both take after your uncle."

Tori's and Sam's eyes popped wide open and their feet hit the floor. It was amazing how being compared to Uncle Leo woke them up. They yanked off their pajamas and quickly dressed like they were hurrying down to open presents under the Christmas tree.

Everyone at our campsite was going fishing except Yolanda and Brady. They said they would watch Bruna.

I snapped the leash to Bruna's collar and walked her over to Yolanda and Abe's pop-up tent. Abe was outside gathering his fishing equipment. I could hear Brady whining inside the tent. "But I want to go fishing!"

Brady wanted to go fishing as much as Sam didn't. They should trade places.

"Hi, Piper," Abe said, giving me a salute. I'd saluted Abe when I first met him and he'd never forgotten.

"Good morning, sir," I said, saluting back.

"Brady isn't too happy about not going fishing," he said.

"Maybe Mom would let him go with us," I told him.

Abe smiled. "Thanks, Piper, but maybe next year Brady can go after a few more swimming lessons."

Brady cried louder, "But I could wear my floaties!"

"I'm a great swimmer," I said. "I'd save Brady if he fell into the water."

"Thanks, Piper, but Yolanda will take him on the dock later."

Yolanda unzipped the tent's opening and slipped out. "Good morning, Piper."

"Top of the morning to you," I told her.

Brady stuck his head through the opening. "Piper, I want to go swimming."

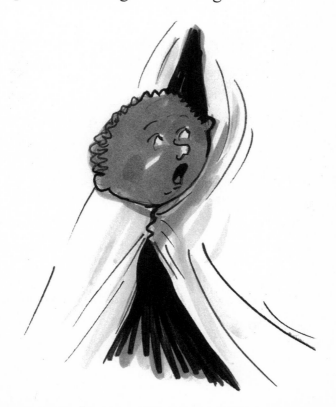

I had to think fast. "But, Brady, who would watch Bruna?"

"Mommy," Brady said.

I cupped my hand around my mouth as if I was telling Brady a secret even though I knew Abe and Yolanda could hear me. "Brady, Bruna might not listen to your mom. She likes you best."

Sometimes that seemed like the truth. Bruna listened to about half of what I said and all of what Brady said.

"Well . . ." Brady stared down, rubbing his chin. Then he looked me straight in the eyes. "Can I be the boss of her?"

"Of your mom?" I asked.

"No, silly. Boona. Can I be the boss of Boona?"

"Yep. Sure thing."

"Can I make her walk on the leash?"

"Mmm-hmm."

"Can I tell her to woll over?"

"Certainly."

"Okay!" Brady said.

Bribing a little kid was exhausting work.

By the time we met at the dock, the sun was just starting to peek above the horizon. It was too early for breakfast, but we waited for Mom and Chief to drink coffee. I didn't mind. Mom without coffee in the morning was not a pretty sight. They quickly drank a cup and then poured the rest of the coffee into two thermoses. Mom took the blue one and Chief took the green.

Everyone gathered on the dock and then divided into small groups. Hailey and Nicole went with Mr. and Mrs. Austin. Michael and Stanley went with Abe and Chief. That meant I was stuck in Mom's boat with my sisters who didn't want to fish. There's nothing worse than being stuck with people who don't want to do something you want to do. Those people were bubble busters.

"Here, Piper," Mom said, "take an oar and make yourself useful."

I took hold of the oar. Mom gave the other one to Tori. We began to row.

"You're going too fast!" Tori yelled.

"Hurry up then, slowpoke," I said, continuing my pace.

"Girls, you need to find a rhythm and stick to it. Piper, slow it down a bit."

"See," Tori said, her eyes turning into slits.

"Tori," Mom said, "pick up the pace a bit."

I didn't say a word. I just smiled.

A few yards away Chief handed Michael an oar while Abe offered one to Stanley.

Stanley shook his head. "No, I better not. I wouldn't be any good. I'm terrible at sailing. Rowing would be the same. If my brother Simon was here, he could do it. He——"

Abe interrupted him, still holding out the oar. "How are you going to know if you don't try?"

Stanley shrugged. "Well, if you say so." He grabbed the oar with such gusto he knocked Abe off balance. Abe tipped to the side, but held on to the edge to keep from falling into the water.

"Sorry about that." Stanley dipped the oar into the water and stirred as if he was cooking a pot of soup.

"Not like that, Stanley," Michael said. "Like this." Michael had been fishing with his dad a lot. He was an expert rower.

"Oh, okay. I get it." Stanley stroked the water with such force that the oar escaped out of his hands and started to float away. Chief grabbed hold of it, just as it was about to be out of reach.

"Oops," Stanley said. "I told you I wouldn't be any good at it. There's not much that I do well. If you would have asked my brother Simon he could have rowed you anywhere you wanted. My brother is an excellent sailor. He's also won trophies for all kinds of things and earned a whole mess of them. . . ."

Simon, Simon, Simon. I was glad we'd rowed our boat away from the guys' boat and I couldn't hear Stanley's gibber about his perfect big brother anymore.

"Let's stop right here," Mom said. She pointed to a log covered with moss that had fallen in the water. "That would be a great place to find fish."

"There aren't any goldfish in that spot, are there?" Sam asked.

"No," Mom said. "Just some perch."

Sam might be a spelling bee prodigy, but she doesn't know much about science. What did she think a lake was? A giant koi pond?

Mom dug in the bait box and pulled out real, live, wiggly worms. She baited Tori's and Sam's hooks, but I wanted to do my own.

My right hand held the hook. My left hand searched in the bait box. When I found a worm, I gently pulled it out. It wiggled and wiggled. I moved the hook toward the worm. But when the hook reached an inch from the worm, I froze. The worm wiggled and wiggled. I could have sworn I heard it squeaking: "Help me, help me!"

I guess I never thought about what happened to a worm once it was on a hook. Now that's all I could think about. It was as if *I* was that worm. The stab. *Ouch, ouch!* The water. *Gurgle, gurgle!* The fish. *Chomp, chomp.*

While I held the worm and the hook, Sam hollered, "I got one! I got a fish!"

Her float bobbed under the water a few times.

"You sure do, Sam," Mom said. "Hold the rod tight." Still seated, Mom scooted to Sam's side and fixed her hands over Sam's. Together, they yanked. Then Mom let go and Sam reeled by herself. Soon a silver fish appeared above the water.

"Now reel him in quickly," Mom told her.

Sam turned the handle. But before she finished, she pointed her rod straight in the air and the fish swung back and forth above our heads. Sam squealed, still reeling.

The fish swung toward me and hit me in the face. I dropped my worm a few inches from Tori's sneakers.

"Ahh!" she screamed.

"It's just a worm," I told her.

Mom grabbed the fish. "It's a beauty, Sam."

Sam rubbed her hands together. "I'm going to eat him!"

I tried to dig for another worm, but my fingertips barely touched the surface of the dirt. Now that I saw what happened to Sam's worm, I felt like a murderer.

Mom watched me. Finally she said, "Piper, why don't you be my guinea pig and try this new bait." She handed me a box. I wondered what was in this one. Crickets? Grasshoppers? Maybe I wasn't cut out for fishing.

"Aren't you going to open the box?" Tori asked.

"Sure, I am." I held my breath. Slowly, I lifted the lid and stared down at the worms—fake worms, red, yellow, and green worms. This was more like it.

The sunrise turned the sky pink and blue. I

heard Bruna barking and I looked toward the dock. Brady and Yolanda were there with her. Yolanda waved to us. Brady held a fishing pole that must have been three times taller than he was.

"Look, Piper," he yelled. "I'm fishing!"

"Get off the bus, Brady!"

"Look, Sam!" he shouted. "I'm fishing!"

"That's great, Brady. Me too. I even caught a big fish."

"Look, Mrs. Reed," Brady hollered. "I'm fishing."

"My, my!" Mom said. "Leave some fish for us, please."

"Okay," Brady said. Then he was quiet.

Tori's tongue made a snapping noise. "What did I ever do to him?"

I cast my fishing line into the lake. "The kid has good instincts."

Suddenly we heard Yolanda yell, "Oh no!"

We looked toward the dock, but she was pointing to the lake. One of the boats had flipped over. Chief, Abe, Michael, and Stanley were in the water, and Stanley was saying, "I'm sorry. I knew I'd be lousy at fishing."

7

Project Stanley

Chief and Abe gathered the oars and flipped the boat back over. Michael swam to the edge and climbed in. I wish Stanley would have been with us. Then I could have gone swimming.

Stanley was still a few yards away from the boat, treading water, the orange life vest framing his head.

Chief held out an oar and told him, "Grab hold, Stanley."

Stanley gripped the oar, and Chief pulled

him toward the boat. Then Abe and Michael helped drag Stanley into the boat.

"I guess Stanley isn't that good at swimming either," Sam said.

Mom's right eyebrow shot up. "Sam, we can't all be good at everything."

"That's true," said Sam, "but I'm good at a bunch of things."

"Like what?" I should have known better than to ask.

Sam gently placed her fishing rod on the floor of the boat and began to count on her fingers. "One, spelling. Two, writing stories. Three, dancing. Four, reading. Five, taking care of Peaches the Second—"

"Peaches the Second is a goldfish!" I told her. "What's the big deal about taking care of a goldfish?"

"It's a very important job," she said.

"And don't forget about Peaches the First," I told her. "God rest her soul."

Tori squinted her eyes at me. "Piper Reed, you are mean."

"Fact is fact," I said.

"Okay, girls, that's enough," Mom said. Then she let out a great big sigh.

Tori shook her head. "It's strange that Stanley isn't good at swimming. His brother Simon is a champion—"

"Stop!" I said, "Don't tell me another thing about Simon. Stanley Hampshire is going to do something wonderful and fabulous before we leave this camp. I'm going to see to it, if it's the last thing I do."

I could hardly believe the words that were coming out of my mouth. One minute ago I was wishing Stanley wasn't a Gypsy Club member, that he wasn't in my class, that he wasn't on our camping trip. Now all I could think about was how I was going to make him shine.

All of a sudden, Sam's fishing pole started moving.

"Get your pole, Sam!"

Sam grabbed hold of her pole and yanked. The red-and-white float bobbed up and down. "Oooo! I think I have a big fish." She pulled and pulled.

Mom helped her reel. The

handle seemed to become harder and harder to turn.

"Oh, my goodness!" Sam said. "It must be really big!"

Figures! I hadn't caught one miserable fish and Sam was on her second. At least Tori hadn't caught any either.

Suddenly Sam's big catch appeared above the water's surface—a great big stick!

"Sam, you forgot something on the things you're good at list," I said. "Six, catching sticks."

Even after the boat turned over, Chief and the guys caught a dozen fish altogether. Although Stanley was quick to point out that he didn't catch any.

By mid-morning, Mom caught two and Tori and I caught one each. Sam caught one fish and two sticks.

"You've got a real knack for that stick catching," I told her.

I was starting to feel sorry for Stanley. "Don't worry," I told him later. "Not everyone can be good at everything. You're good at something."

"If you say so," Stanley said. "I just wish I knew what that was."

I was starting to wonder, too. What could it be? It wasn't sailing, swimming, fishing, or making a campfire. But that left a lot of things. Now I just had to think of them.

After we got back from fishing, Chief, Abe, and Michael's dad cleaned the fish. "Do you want to learn to clean fish, Stanley?"

"Not really. I have a queasy stomach."

He wasn't the only one with a queasy stomach. Nicole was feeling sick. "I wonder if I'm allergic to fishing," she said.

Mrs. Austin told her to go lie down in their trailer. After she checked on Nicole, she came back out. "She has a bit of a fever. Could Hailey stay with you?" she asked Mom.

"Of course," Mom said. "Do you think it could be serious?"

"I'm going to keep an eye on her. But right now I don't want to get alarmed. She might've just gotten overexcited."

Mrs. Austin was a lieutenant, but she always said, "I'm a mom first."

Once Chief overheard her say that, and he said, "Yep, and I'm a dad first."

"Piper," Chief called out. "Do me a favor? Could you put these cleaned fish in the ice chest near the Airstream?"

"Sure," I said, then I had a great idea. I'd let Stanley do it. It was a small job, but maybe it would build his confidence. Accomplishing a small task could lead to a bigger one.

I took the plastic bags of fish from Chief. Then I hollered to Stanley. "Stanley, could you do an important favor for me?"

"Me?"

"Yes, you. Could you put these bags of fish in the ice chest by our camper? It's really important. We're going to have them for dinner."

"Are you sure you trust me to do that?"

"Absolutely."

Stanley pushed at the bridge of his glasses, then reluctantly took the bags. I pointed to our trailer and left him.

I felt better already. Building up Stanley was going to be a lot easier than I thought. Every time I had something important to do, I'd pass the job to him. Soon he would be walking proud. Soon no one would care about Simon Hampshire. Everyone would be talking about Stanley.

"Piper," Mom said, "don't forget about Bruna."

I started to walk over to Yolanda, but then I noticed Stanley had returned from his first task. "Stanley, could you go get Bruna from Yolanda?"

"Your dog?" Stanley asked.

"Yep."

"I like your dog."

"That's why I thought you might want to help keep an eye on her for me."

"Sure." Stanley walked away, heading toward Yolanda's tent where Bruna's leash was attached to the picnic table.

He brought Bruna back to me. "Gee, thanks, Stanley. I really appreciate it."

"No big deal," he said.

He was right. It really wasn't a big deal to fetch Bruna from Yolanda and walk her a few yards. But it was another little step in building up Stanley.

8

No Easy Job

"Is everyone ready for the nature hike?" Mom asked.

Brady rose on his tiptoes "Yes!" Then he whispered, "Will we see any bears?"

"Let's hope not," Tori said. "I didn't sign on for any bear hunt."

"Well, I did," I said. Then I chanted, "I'm going on a bear hunt."

Sam joined in, then Brady. Soon we were all walking and singing about going on a bear hunt. Even Tori joined in. And when she did, Brady said to her, "You're silly."

Tori stopped singing and looked down at him.

Then Brady smiled up at her. "I like silly."

Brady stretched out his hand to her and Tori took hold of it. Together they began again, "I'm going on a bear hunt."

Walking through the woods may not sound very interesting, but Mom and Abe both knew a lot about plants and birds and they made it like a treasure hunt. Mom must have pointed out eight different woodpeckers. Maybe she had more in common with Uncle Leo than she wanted to admit.

Before we knew it, Chief announced, "We'd better return to the campsite and get started on dinner. I can almost taste those perch."

"How are you going to cook them?" Yolanda asked.

"The best way," Chief said. "The only way—fried."

"You can take the boy out of Louisiana," said Mom, "but you can't take Louisiana out of the boy." Mom and Chief grew up in Piney Woods, Louisiana, population 492. And both our grandmothers believed in the same cooking motto: *If it ain't fried, it ain't cooked.*

It would have been a perfect day, if Nicole hadn't gotten sick. Just as I was heading to her trailer window, Chief yelled, "Piper! Piper Reed!"

I knew that tone. It was not the *Piper Reed, you are an outstanding camper* tone. It was not the *Piper Reed, don't tell your sisters, but you are our favorite kid* tone. It was the *Piper Reed, you're in trouble* tone. But I had no idea why. I swung around and saluted. "Yes, sir?"

"Get over here."

I rushed to where Chief was standing next

to the ice chest. It was open and it was empty.

"I thought I told you to put the fish in the ice chest."

"I did. I mean, Stanley did."

"What do you mean *Stanley did*? I asked you to do it."

Stanley stood by, studying the ground, his eyes darting about as if he was following an ant.

Chief folded his arms across his chest. "The fish are gone, Piper."

My face burned. "Stanley, didn't you put the fish in the ice chest?"

Stanley slowly raised his chin. "In? You said *in*? I thought you said *on* the ice chest."

Chief started scouting around the campsite. I decided to help him. Maybe Mrs. Austin noticed the bags of fish on top of the ice chest and put them in theirs. But as I was about to go ask her, I found a plastic bag caught on a lower tree branch. An empty plastic bag. Then Chief found the other one. There had been only two bags, but he kept searching, brushing the ground with his hand.

"Just as I suspected," he said. "Raccoons."

"What?"

"See." He pointed to their tracks on the ground.

"Get off the bus!" I'd never seen raccoon tracks. "Can I take a picture of them?"

Chief frowned. I guess finding something as cool as raccoon tracks didn't matter when the raccoons ate your dinner.

Sam trotted over to us. "Did the raccoon eat *my* fish?"

"Of course, Sam," I told her. "They didn't know you were special."

Stanley didn't say a word. He just dug his heel in the dirt.

Brady walked over and squatted for a closer view of the tracks. "I want to eat fwied fish."

Stanley moved away from all of us like he was trying to disappear. He walked toward the dock.

I took off after him. I was looking forward

to Chief's fried fish and hush puppies, too. But I felt sorry for Stanley. Now I was going to have to work extra hard to build him up.

When I met him on the dock, he was throwing stones into the water.

"I'm really sorry. I guess I messed up big this time."

"It's okay, Stanley. You didn't mess up big. You only messed up by one word. On and in. In and on. They sound so much alike. And really you only messed up by one letter."

Stanley looked up at me. "Gee, Piper. You're a good friend."

I'd had a lot of friends in my life, but I never had any of them tell me that. I was trying to make Stanley feel good about himself and he surprised me and made me feel good.

Mom joined us on the dock. "Stanley, please don't worry. This means we'll have Just in Case Stew tonight."

"Just in case?" I asked.

"Just in Case We Don't Catch Enough Fish Stew. I bought ingredients to make a batch."

Although I guess in this situation it should be called Just in Case the Raccoons Eat Our Fish Stew.

Mom and Yolanda cooked some ground beef in a big pot. Then they added vegetables—corn, beans, peas, carrots. I hated to admit it, but dinner smelled delicious. Fishing and hiking were like swimming. They made me hungry. And even though we didn't have fish, Chief still fried his famous hush puppies.

After dinner, we fixed s'mores with chocolate bars and toasted marshmallows and graham crackers. At least raccoons didn't eat marshmallows.

This was the best camping trip ever. I'd

almost forgotten about Halloween. "Hey, what about tomorrow?"

"What about tomorrow?" Mom asked as if she had no idea, but I could tell she was just teasing. "Is there anything special going on tomorrow?"

"Halloween!" Brady and Sam said together.

I hoped Stanley didn't ruin Halloween. If

Stanley couldn't do a simple task like putting fish in the ice chest, I don't know how he could get through Halloween without messing up something. I had other things to worry about though. I still hadn't figured out what my Halloween costume was going to be.

9

CAMPSITE HALLOWEEN

After breakfast on Halloween morning, Mom surprised us. She gave each of us a pumpkin and a black marker.

"Real jack-o'-lanterns are supposed to be carved," I told her.

It was amazing how Mom could send a warning with her eyebrows. She didn't have to say a word.

I quickly added, "But there's a lot to be said about being original."

Sam studied her pumpkin and then she announced, "I'm going to make a pr—"

"Don't tell me," I said. "A princess."

Sam frowned. "Wrong! I'm going to make a pr—"

"A prince," I said.

"No!" Sam let out a heavy sigh. "I'm going to make a *pretty* goldfish just like Peaches the Second."

"Sam, how are you going to make a goldfish from a pumpkin?"

"Just wait," she said as she drew long eyelashes on the pumpkin.

Mom asked Hailey and me to carry a pumpkin over to the Austins' trailer for Nicole. She was still sick.

"How is Nicole?" I asked Mrs. Austin.

"She said her throat feels a little itchy." Mrs. Austin turned to Hailey. "Are you feeling ill, Hailey? You were in the boat with her yesterday."

"No. My mom says I have a strong immune system. I've never even had a cold."

"Everyone has had a cold," I said.

"Well, I haven't," said Hailey. She always had to be the best at everything.

We returned to the group and worked on on our pumpkins. When we were finished, we had three smiling jack-o'-lanterns, a laughing jack-o'-lantern, two scary jack-o'-lanterns, and a goldfish. We also had a jack-o'-lantern covered with lots of scribbles.

"My jacky-latwen is silly!" Brady said, pointing to it and bursting into a fit of giggles.

I grinned at him.

"You crack yourself up, don't you, Brady?"

"Yep."

I paid special attention to Stanley's. If there was ever a smug jack-o'-lantern, Stanley had drawn one. The right corner of the pumpkin's mouth turned up into a smirk.

"My jack-o'-lantern is named Simon," said Stanley.

At the mere mention of Simon's name, Tori's head swung in the direction of Stanley's pumpkin. When she noticed the snotty grin, she frowned.

"It looks just like him," Stanley said.

"You mean your brother has a pumpkin head?" I asked.

Stanley nodded. "Yeah, I would say so."

By lunchtime I knew what my costume was going to be. I had brown pants and a brown T-shirt in my suitcase, just right for an apple tree. We'd brought more than enough apples for the apple-bobbing game. Now I just needed a bunch of leaves.

I started to take off for my leaf gathering when Tori yelled, "Piper Reed, don't forget Bruna! It's your turn."

Tori walked over with Bruna. She slapped the leash in my hand and dug in her pocket. "Here are the L-I-V-E-R L-U-M-P-S," she spelled.

"Liver Lumps!" Sam yelled. She could never resist showing off her reading skills.

Bruna barked and wagged her tail. I gave her a Liver Lump. Then we started on the trail.

"Don't go alone," Mom called out from the Airstream window.

"I'm not. Bruna is with me."

"Take a friend, and don't go too far."

At her trailer window, Nicole called out, "I'd go with you, Piper, if I weren't sick."

"How are you feeling today?" I asked.

"Better, but not a hundred percent."

Nearby, Hailey was writing on a piece of paper.

I went over to her. "Do you want to walk with me?"

Hailey didn't even look up. "I've got to finish my homework. My mom said if I went camping, I had to make sure I finished it."

Mom overheard and asked, "Do you have homework, Piper?"

"Nah, I don't have any." It was true. I didn't have any homework with me. I left out the part about forgetting to bring it. I rushed off so she didn't have a chance to ask more questions.

Michael couldn't go either. He had to help his dad collect wood for that night's fire.

Stanley was sitting under a tree, listening to Sam read her book to him. Nicole was at the window listening, too. I could tell Nicole was interested even though she had her own copy of *Princess Samantha, Ruler of the Fair Land of NAS Pensacola*. But Stanley was digging his heel in the dirt. He'd made a pretty big hole, probably looking for a way to escape underground.

"Hey, Stanley," I yelled, "do you want to walk with me?"

Stanley jumped to his feet. A grin spread across his face.

Sam stared up, frowning. "He's listening to my story."

Stanley's shoulders slumped as he sat down.

"Mom said I can't walk by myself," I told her. "He can hear your story later."

"I promise I will," Stanley said, standing once again.

"When?" Sam asked.

"Before we go back home," said Stanley.

"I want to hear the rest," Nicole said.

Stanley and I walked quickly away.

"Don't you love Halloween, Stanley?"

"Yep, I do."

We walked along the trail and I started picking leaves from trees on the lower branches and Stanley helped. Most of the leaves hung from higher branches that we couldn't reach.

"Trick-or-treating is my favorite thing to do on Halloween," said Stanley. "Are we going to trick-or-treat?"

"Well, there are only two trailers and a pop-up tent at our campsite. And I don't think the parents are going to let us go to the other campsites."

"I like to trick-or-treat until my sack fills up. Then I go home and dump it and go back for some more."

"You're not supposed to go back to the same houses, Stanley."

"I didn't know there were any official Halloween rules."

"I guess there aren't any official rules. It's just one of those things everyone knows."

Stanley shrugged. "If you say so."

Most of the leaves were on branches that towered above our heads, but soon we discovered a patch of vines wrapped around the trunk and growing on the ground at the foot of the tree.

"Look!" Stanley pointed at the vine.

"Great find, Stanley! See, your Boy Scout skills have come in handy."

"Those leaves look familiar," said Stanley, "but I can't remember why."

Each leaf had three points and there were plenty of them. We picked and picked until we filled up the sack. Then we headed back.

"That was easy," Stanley said.

"Thanks to you," I told him.

Stanley held his head high as we made our way back to camp.

My hands began to itch. "I wish I'd used insect

repellant before we left." I scratched, and when I did, the itchy feeling traveled up my wrists.

"Me, too." Stanley dug his fingernails into his arms.

"Those were sneaky bugs. They attacked and left before I got a glimpse of them. Did you see them?"

"Nope," Stanley said. "I wonder if it was a brown recluse spider. Simon said a brown recluse is very tiny but if they bite, you could lose a body part."

I counted my fingers. They were all there. But they sure did itch.

After lunch, I took a needle and thread from Mom's sewing kit and sewed each leaf onto my T-shirt. Then I tripled the thread and tied it around the stem of the apples, attaching them to the T-shirt and my baseball cap. Now not only did my hands and wrists itch, but so did

my forearms. By the time I was finished sewing on the leaves, my entire arms felt like I'd been bitten by a bunch of brown recluse spiders. I sure hoped I didn't lose both of my arms. If I did, how would I ever be a Blue Angel pilot?

When it was time to put on my costume, my arms and hands were covered in red dots. I tried hard not to scratch, but it was useless.

I decided not to say anything. If my parents suspected I'd been bitten by a brown recluse I'd probably have to go to the hospital. At the very least, I'd be stuck in the trailer like Nicole. That was no way to spend Halloween. I went outside to join my friends.

Stanley wore a Superman costume. "Hey, Super Stanley!" I said.

"I'm Superman," he told me.

"I like Super Stanley better," I told him.

Stanley pushed at his glasses. "It's Halloween. I can pretend to be who I want."

Michael was dressed as a dill pickle, his favorite food. "How are you doing, Dill?"

"Not so sweet," Michael said.

"Hardy-har-har," I said. "I thought you'd sour for Halloween."

"Are you an apple tree?" asked Stanley.

"Yes," I stood tall and stretched my arms to the side. A few apples hung from my sleeves.

"Oh." He didn't sound impressed. Suddenly my idea didn't seem as fabulous as I thought it was. And I was itching like crazy. It seemed to get worse after I put on my costume.

Even though Hailey wasn't feeling well, she wore her mom's lieutenant uniform shirt and hat and waved to us from the open window. Dressed in his crown and cape, Prince Brady settled next to Princess Elizabeth.

Our parents pulled out the lawn chairs and sat. It was time for the costume parade. Sam and Brady were first. I wish I'd been first. That way I could get out of my itchy costume.

"Princess Elizabeth and Prince Brady!" Tori announced in her anchorwoman's voice. I liked how Tori thought she was too old for trick-or-treat, but didn't want to miss out on all the fun.

"Pwince Billy Bob," Brady said.

"Billy Bob?" Sam was not pleased. "There is no Prince Billy Bob."

"Yep," Brady said. "That's me."

They walked together in front of the parents. Brady held his crown as he inched carefully by, but Sam had lots of practice with a crown on her head. She pranced a few steps in front of him. I guess Princess Elizabeth didn't want to be caught walking side by side with a prince named Billy Bob.

"Mr. Dill Pickle," Tori called out with a wave of her arm.

Michael wiggled as he walked, a kind of pickle dance, I guessed.

When Michael finished, Tori said, "Is it a bird?"

Everyone yelled, "No!"

"Is it a plane?"

"No!"

"There's no need to fear. Superman is here!"

Stanley climbed atop the picnic table, jumped, and flexed his skinny biceps. Then he stretched out his arms and ran by the adults, stopping just short of a tree. Blue sleeves hid his arms, but I could see his pink polka-dotted hands. I looked down at my hands. They were covered with the same pink dots. So were my arms. I hummed "Yankee Doodle" to try and keep my mind off the itching.

"An apple tree," said Tori. She said it as if she was having to fight off a yawn.

My body itched all over. I continued to hum. I felt like twirling to keep from wanting to scratch. Then I had an idea. I wasn't just an apple tree.

"Apple tree in a tornado," I whispered to Tori.

"Huh?" She wrinkled her nose. "Okay. Apple tree in a TORNADO."

I closed my eyes and hummed "Yankee Doodle." I twirled and twirled. The apples fell off to the ground with a thump. Get off the bus! I was like a real tornado.

Even though I was dizzy, I peeked, trying to see Chief's reaction. His mouth dropped open. "Piper, what on earth did you get into?"

I stopped and tried to focus. Everything and everyone was still spinning. The lake looked like it flew into the sky. I fell to the ground.

"Are those real leaves?" Abe asked, standing above me.

"Yep. Stanley and I found them on the trail."

Mom bent over and took a close look. She gasped. "Piper! That's poison ivy all over your costume! Get out of those clothes quick!"

At first I froze. Then I rushed into the trailer

and shed my clothes. From inside, I heard Stanley say, "I knew there was something familiar about those leaves. We learned about poison ivy in Boy Scouts."

Then Abe hollered, "Stanley, you must have gotten into it, too. Run to our tent and change."

Mom put on Chief's work gloves and threw my apple tree clothes and hat in a garbage sack. She spread pink lotion over my arms and hands. She made me swallow some medicine for the infection. And then she took the lotion and medicine over to Abe so that he could help Stanley. His parents' note said he wasn't allergic to anything. It was a good thing his name wasn't Nicole Austin.

A few minutes later, dressed in plain clothes, Stanley and I joined the others. That was the quickest amount of time I had ever worn a Halloween costume.

Suddenly Sam said, "I know what Piper and Stanley are."

"What?" I asked.

"Pink polka-dot monsters with the creepy crawly disease."

Everyone laughed. I was just glad the pink lotion made most of the itching go away.

Later we bobbed for apples. When it got dark, we sat in a circle around the fire and listened to Tori tell scary stories. Only they weren't scary.

"She opened the door and BOO!" Tori said. But Brady and Sam grabbed hands and squealed. Even Nicole squealed. From her window.

Just when I thought I couldn't take another of Tori's boring stories, something hit my head. Worms! It was raining big glowing worms. We all screamed then. Until we discovered Chief and Abe up in the tree above us.

Then we went trick-or-treating. When we knocked on the Airstream door, Mom and

Chief answered. Mom wore a witch's hat and a cat mask covered Chief's face.

At the tent, Yolanda and Abe were dressed like a caveman and cavewoman.

Mr. and Mrs. Austin wore cowboy hats. "Howdy, partners," they said, tipping their hats.

After they dropped candy in our bags, I glanced down in my sack. This was the puniest amount of candy I'd ever got on Halloween. Then I announced, "Hey, maybe we should trick-or-treat Stanley style."

Everyone followed Stanley and me as we rushed back to the Airstream. We held our sacks out, ready to shout, "Trick or treat!"

The door slowly opened, and to our surprise, a ghost stood there.

"Ahh!" we yelled, jumping back.

"Aw, it's only Tori under a sheet," I said. But secretly I wanted to yell "Get off the bus!"

My sister had actually surprised me, only for a second, though.

Yolanda and Abe became firemen on their second round. The Austins put on redbird masks. We returned, again and again, to the trailers and tent, never knowing who we'd find behind the doors. It really felt like we were trick-or-treating at different homes. Only it was better.

Suddenly Mom said, "Piper, where is Bruna?"

I jumped up and gasped. "Bruna!"

The last time I'd seen her was hours ago when I was still an apple tree and Stanley was still Super Stanley.

10

Calling Bruna

Little beams from our flashlights bounced against the woods.

"Bruna! Bruna!" We called out.

"Boona," cried Brady.

We were all there except for Nicole and Mrs. Austin who stayed behind at the campsite.

My heart felt like it had dropped into my stomach. It was my fault. I was in charge of Bruna. I'd been the one to convince Mom and

Chief to let her come camping with us. Now she was lost.

I thought about the day we went to pick her up at the poodle lady's house. I'd wanted a German shepherd instead of a poodle until I saw those little floppy ears and her bobbed tail with a pom-pom. I thought about how she slept with me and kept my cold feet warm at the foot of the bed. I thought about the tricks I'd taught her and how we almost won the Gypsy Club Pet Show. A big lump lodged in my throat. It was so big, I couldn't even call out her name.

The wind blew through the tree branches and made a crackle sound. Above our heads I heard a *hoot-hoot*.

"What's that?" asked Sam.

"An owl," Mom said. Then she and Sam went back to calling, "Bruna! Bruna!"

A thin cloud drifted in front of a full moon. It felt like a Halloween night with all the eerie sounds and sights. Now I really was scared. I was scared for Bruna.

That big knot in my throat kept me from joining in with the others. Then I noticed Stanley wasn't calling her name either. He was fiddling with the flashlight, turning it on and off.

I walked closer to him.

"I'm thinking," Stanley said.

"About what?" I asked.

"Bruna. You know if I was a dog, it might scare me if a whole bunch of people were yelling my name. I'd think I was in trouble."

Stanley had a point. He continued explaining. "And if I was a dog out exploring in the woods, having a fun time, I'd have to have a real good reason to stop."

"Yes?"

Stanley shined his flashlight under his chin so that his entire face glowed. "What does Bruna like better than anything in the whole world?"

I thought hard, trying to think of what it was that Bruna liked the most. I slipped my hands in my pockets. That's when I knew.

Then above everyone's voices calling out "Bruna!" I yelled, "Get off the bus!"

Every flashlight turned toward me. It was so bright I covered my eyes until they pointed them to the ground.

"What's wrong, Piper?" Chief asked.

"I have a great idea. I mean Stanley has a great idea."

"You're kidding," Hailey said.

"No." I frowned at her and continued. "It's a really, really great idea. Stanley said we should think about what Bruna wants more than anything in the world."

"And just what would that be?" Tori asked.

"Liver Lumps!" I said.

Mom nodded, smiling. "Great idea, Stanley. Piper, why don't you give it a try? And the rest of us will keep quiet."

I took a deep breath and yelled at the top of my voice. So loud that everyone covered their ears. "Bruna, Liver Lump! Liver Lump, Bruna! Liver Lump, Liver Lump!"

We began to walk again, the light from our flashlights dotting the trail. My voice was the only one, calling, "Liver Lump, Bruna." I made sure to make my voice sound happy like Bruna had done something good even though running away was bad. Still we couldn't blame her for wanting to explore. She was a dog, after all.

My arms felt itchy again. I scratched and scratched as we walked and walked. I was starting to think Stanley's brilliant idea wasn't so brilliant. That big knot came back and my eyes went all blurry. I didn't want to know what it was like to not have Bruna in my life. But it looked like I was going to have to find out.

Then I heard a bark. A familiar bark. Sam covered her mouth with both hands, but she jumped up and down. Brady joined her, covering his mouth, too.

Soon we heard some bushes rustling. We pointed our flashlights in the direction of the shaking bush. And then we saw the little floppy ears, the bobbed tail with the pom-pom.

Get off the bus!

Bruna walked over to me and sat. Dried leaves stuck to her coat. She looked up.

I patted her head. "Good girl."

She stood and wagged her tail.

"Good girl," I said again.

She barked.

"What's wrong, Bruna?" I asked.

Then our entire group of campers yelled, "She wants a Liver Lump!"

"Genius," muttered Tori.

"Oh, I knew that." I dug in my pocket and pulled out five Liver Lumps. And although I usually gave her only one or two a day, this time, I gave her every one of them. It was Halloween, after all.

And it was the best Halloween ever—poison ivy and pink polka dots and finding Bruna. And it wouldn't have happened without Stanley's great idea. Finally Stanley could do something special that none of us could do. Not even his pumpkin head brother Simon. Stanley Hampshire could think like a dog!

11

HAPPY TRAILS

While Chief cooked pancakes for breakfast the next morning, I took paper, scissors, and markers, and made something for Stanley. The idea came to me after we found Bruna. Michael and Hailey agreed we should do it.

I gobbled down three pancakes. Then I put Bruna on her leash and together we walked to the lake. After what happened last night, I didn't want her out of my sight.

The Gypsy Club met me on the dock. Nicole

must have gotten better because she was there, too.

"Today we have a special presentation for our newest member—Stanley Hampshire."

Stanley's eyes popped wide. "Me? Gosh, what did I do that was so special? I mean I'm not saying that I don't want to have a special presentation, but I just can't possibly think of what I could have done to deserve this. I—"

My hand went up, the palm facing him. "Stanley!"

"What?"

"Be quiet." Then I added. "Please."

"If you say so," Stanley said.

I cleared my throat. "Stanley, as founder of the Gypsy Club, I'm proud to present our very first badge to you."

"A badge," Stanley started. "I can—"

I held up my palm and he pressed his lips together tight.

Then I held up the badge. "Stanley, you have earned the Think Like a Dog badge. If it weren't for your suggestion, we might never have found Bruna. It was a simple idea, but most great ideas are. Why, look at the invention of Velcro. That came about because of some grass burrs sticking to a man's clothing. Just think if that simple idea had never happened and look at—"

Hailey sighed and showed me her palm.

"Okay," I said. "Anyway, Stanley, you deserve this badge. If you hadn't thought of that idea, I would have never said *Liver Lump*."

Bruna barked and wiggled her tail.

"And," I continued, but Hailey interrupted.

"That's right," she said. "We're proud of you, Stanley."

"I'm proud of you, too," said Nicole.

"Just remember," Michael said, "I was the one who invited him to the Gypsy Club."

"You don't get a badge for that," I told him.

I pinned the badge on Stanley's shirt and we all saluted him. Then I counted, "One, two, three!" And we all said, "Get off the bus, Stanley Hampshire!"

An hour later we formed our caravan. The Austins first, then Brady's family, then us. When we arrived in Yazoo, Alabama, everyone else drove on while we waited for Uncle Leo in the post office parking lot.

"I wonder if Uncle Leo will get lost again," said Sam.

"Probably," Mom said.

Chief smiled at her and she laughed.

"I have an idea," I said. "It worked once before."

"What?" Tori asked.

"We could holler Liver Lump."

"Hardy-har-har," said Tori.

Just then we spotted Uncle Leo's car coming down the road.

"He's bound to see us now," Chief said. "We've got the Airstream."

But Uncle Leo drove right on by, not even glancing our way.

Chief groaned. "Oh, no!"

All of us jumped out of the car, getting ready for him to pass again. This time we knew better than to call his name.

I had a hunch about what would work. Thank goodness Uncle Leo's car window was down. When he made a U-turn and headed back, I cupped my hands around my mouth and hollered, "Hummingbird!"

Then, all of us, even Chief hollered, "Hum-mingbird! Hummingbird!"

Uncle Leo screeched on the brakes, stopping

in time to make the turn into the parking lot. He pulled up next to us.

"Did anyone say hummingbird?" he asked, staring as if he was expecting us to hand over a stripe-tailed one.

Stanley Hampshire's genius idea had worked again! But I don't even think Stanley would want a Think-Like-an-Uncle-Leo badge.

Later, back in our car, I said, "It's too bad Uncle Leo doesn't have a cell phone anymore."

Sam leaned forward. "Daddy, can I use your cell phone? I have an important call to make."

Chief chuckled. "Sounds very important." He handed his phone to Sam.

"What's Mrs. Austin's cell phone number?" Sam asked.

Mom told the number and Sam began to dial. "Hi, Mrs. Austin. May I please speak to Stanley?"

Sam opened her copy of *Princess Samantha, Ruler of the Fair Land of NAS Pensacola* and began to read. "Then the princess thought about all the people on the base . . ."

I sighed. Maybe there shouldn't be a Think-Like-an-Uncle-Leo badge, but after this, Stanley definitely deserved a Surviving-Sam's-Story badge!